OUT OF BREATH:
Kendra's Big Secret

ILLUSTRATED BY ZOË GATTI

BY DESTINEY MAYHEW, ADEREMI ABOSEDE & KAIRON CUNNINGHAM

Reach Incorporated | Washington, DC

Shout Mouse Press

Reach Education, Inc. / Shout Mouse Press
Published by
Shout Mouse Press, Inc.

Shout Mouse Press is a nonprofit writing program and publishing house for
unheard voices. This book was produced through Shout Mouse workshops
and in collaboration with Shout Mouse artists and editors.

Shout Mouse Press empowers writers from marginalized communities to
tell their own stories in their own voices and, as published authors, to act as
agents of change. In partnership with other nonprofit organizations serving
communities in need, we are building a catalog of inclusive, mission-driven
books that engage reluctant readers as well as open hearts and minds.

Learn more and see our full catalog at www.shoutmousepress.org.

For kids who have asthma,
who struggle with low self esteem,
or who follow their dreams
even when others say they can't succeed.

We believe that kids can overcome any struggle.

Kendra the Kangaroo did not want to be at school today. Last night her hockey team lost. AGAIN. And everybody thought it was her fault. AGAIN.

Why me? she wondered. *Why do they have to make fun of my big feet and short arms? Why do they tell me kangaroos don't belong on the ice? If they knew I had asthma, too, they would kick me off the team for sure. I can never tell them.*

She sighed and hopped to class.

Kendra entered class with her head down, but she could feel the anger in the air. She hopped to her seat and heard a lot of whispering.

"Ooh, look who it is! It's the worst player on our team," said Helena the Hyena.

"Yeah, that tail of hers is always getting in my way," said Anton the Ape.

Kendra ignored them and took her seat. To hide her tears, she put her head down on her desk. At moments like this, Kendra felt helpless. She couldn't wait for lunch so she could talk to her best friend.

Math class felt like forever, but finally it was time for lunch. Kendra entered the cafeteria and saw her best friend Rahim the Rabbit sitting at a table. She made three sad, slow hops over to him. "Why the long face, KK?" asked Rahim.

Kendra began to tear up again. "Everyone's saying it was my fault we lost. Now I don't even want to play on Friday."

"That's crazy," said Rahim. "You have to play! It's against Rosedale! Plus, you have the best skills on the team."

Rahim's words made Kendra get hype, but she was still worried.

"Don't sweat it, Kendra," said Rahim. "You should just tell them the truth. Why don't you let them know that you slowed down because of your asthma?"

"No way," said Kendra. "I don't want to tell them the truth. Then they'll NEVER let me play."

Rahim sighed and shook his head, but Kendra didn't care. She did not want to tell. Instead she got ready for practice, and promised herself she would just work harder than everyone else.

The coach blew the whistle and the team started to do skating drills.

Helena the Hyena said, "Watch Coach not make KK do the drills as long as us."

China the Cheetah said, "Yeah, I wonder what makes her so special."

As they continued their drills, Kendra thought, *At least Coach knows what I'm going through.*

After practice, Coach told all the teammates to go change. He added, "Kendra, why don't you hop over here. I want to talk to you for a second."

Kendra thought, *Oh no, what is he calling me in for? Was I not playing well enough?*

As she hopped to the Coach's office, she overheard Anton the Ape saying, "Why doesn't that outback clown quit this team already?"

Coach said, "Kendra, take a seat. I need to talk to you about something. You need to tell your teammates about your asthma so they won't be on your tail so much."

Kendra responded, "I just don't want them to see me as a lesser animal because of something I can't control."

"I understand," said Coach. "But I want what's best for you. I want you to be safe and to have fun. I think you have great potential to be the first real kangaroo hockey star."

"I know you're concerned, but it's something I'd rather not reveal," said Kendra. "Don't worry, Coach, I can handle it."

Kendra quickly hopped away.

When Friday finally arrived, you could feel the rivalry in the air. The tension was live.

The announcer shouted, "Good afternoon! And welcome, everyone, to today's big game between Reach Middle School and Rosedale!"

Kendra felt the tightness in her chest, like her heart would explode. She thought, *I'm going to go out and give it my all. I refuse to let my team down. Today I will prove them wrong.*

The whistle blew and Kendra took her position at the center of the rink for the faceoff. She stared down Penny the Panda and waited for the puck to hit the ice. When it did, Kendra was quick, but Penny was quicker.

"Come on!" yelled Helena the Hyena.

It was a fast-paced game. Rosedale raced down the rink, and then Reach Middle raced right back the other way. There was no time for rest. As Kendra chased down the puck, she could already feel it getting harder to breathe. But if she slowed down, what might her teammates think? Kendra skated faster and pushed herself harder.

The clock ticked down to the end of the first period. China the Cheetah passed the puck way down the rink to Kendra, who stopped it with her extra-long tail. She neared the goal and set herself up to shoot. She could feel her chest getting tighter. She shot the puck, but she missed by an inch.

"Aw man!" she heard her teammates say. "She was so close. She could have scored!"

By the end of second period the score was 1-1. It had been a hard fought game, with one goal from Helena the Hyena, and one from Tim the Tiger for Rosedale.

During the final break, Coach Bear told them it was time to bring it home. Anton the Ape beat his paws against his chest in agreement, Helena the Hyena cackled, and Elijah the Eagle screeched.

Kendra was so tired. She knew that it was time to take a puff of her inhaler, but there was no way to do it without her teammates seeing her.

"Are you OK?" Coach Bear asked her.

"Yeah, I'm fine, Coach!" she lied.

At the final faceoff, Kendra was wheezing. Penny the Panda said, "I'm going to chew you like bamboo." Kendra flicked the puck with her tail and raced down the rink.

She passed Fiona the Frog, who croaked at her, Calvin the Cow, who mooed at her, and finally Ozzy the Octopus, who reached for her with a tentacle, and missed!

As Kendra passed the Rosedale players, she heard her team cheering her on. "Go, KK!"

She moved faster on the ice, even adding in some hops. She wasn't going to let her team down this time.

But just as she came close to the goal and was about to shoot…

Kendra was gripped with panic.
She hit the ice, doubled over from her lack of breath.
She couldn't move.
She gasped and gasped and struggled for air.

The players on the ice stopped skating, and the crowd froze in shock. Coach Bear came onto the ice to help Kendra off.

He said, "Are you ok? I knew you looked tired. Why didn't you tell me? Let's get your inhaler."

Coach Bear carried her off the ice while the whole crowd watched.

Kendra took a puff of her inhaler but felt so sad. She knew her teammates would never see her the same again.

Then Kendra heard Elijah the Eagle shout, "Let's bring it home for Kendra!"

The rest of her teammates cheered.

"We got you, Kendra Kangaroo!" Helena shouted.

The whole crowd cheered, and Kendra could hear her friend Rahim cheering the loudest.

On the rink, China the Cheetah raced as fast as she could down the ice, ducking and dodging the other players. The clock was ticking down.

She passed to Elijah the Eagle, who passed to Helena the Hyena, who passed to Anton the Ape, who finally shot and …

SCORED!

The crowd went wild, shouting and holding up signs, just as the buzzer went off. Reach Middle School WON!

Back in the locker room, the team huddled. Kendra was feeling better. To her surprise, her teammates were smiling at her.

Kendra said, "I was afraid you would judge me if you knew I had asthma, since you guys already teased me so much."

Anton the Ape said, "We're sorry about that. We thought you got special treatment from coach, but now we understand it's because of something out of your control."

Elijah the Eagle screeched, "You never have to put yourself at risk. Your teammates are here for you."

China the Cheetah said, "At the end of the day, we care more about our teammates than about winning the game."

They all high-tailed each other, and the animals without tails smacked paws.

Finally, Kendra felt like part of the team.

About the Authors

ADEREMI ABOSEDE

is seventeen years old and goes to KIPP College Preparatory School. He likes to read, sketch, catch up on political news, help others, and be a well-rounded and intellectual person. He is also the co-author of a Reach book called *The Blue Spark*. He hopes his readers learn that despite personal struggles, individuals can overcome obstacles and understand people.

KAIRON CUNNINGHAM

is sixteen years old and in the eleventh grade. He likes to hang out with friends and play basketball and football. He wrote this book because it seemed like something fun to do and he wanted to see what it was like. He hopes his readers learn that if you love something you should go out and give it your all and strive for greatness.

DESTINEY MAYHEW

is eighteen years old and a senior at Anacostia High School. Her hobby is working with young children because kids are the future. This is not her first book; she wrote a book last year called *Taking Down Ms. Moody*. She wrote this book to inspire children. We all have problems, but we are all able to get through them.

ANDREA MIRVISS and EVA SHAPIRO served as Story Scribes for this book.
KATHY CRUTCHER served as Story Coach and Series Editor.

About the Illustrator

ZOË GATTI

is an illustrator, graphic designer, web designer and photographer based in Brooklyn, NY and Washington, DC. She is currently pursuing a BFA at Pratt Institute in Communications Design with a concentration in Illustration and a minor in Creative Writing. Her passions include narrative illustration, freelance illustration, medical illustration, animation, and photography, both digital and darkroom. She is a graduate of DC's Duke Ellington School of the Arts. You can see her work at www.zoegatti.com

Writers and artists at work

Acknowledgments

For the fourth summer in a row, teens from Reach Incorporated were issued a challenge: compose original children's books that will both educate and entertain young readers. Specifically, these teens were asked to create inclusive stories that reflect the realities of their communities, so that every child has the opportunity to relate to characters on the page. And for the fourth summer in a row, these teens have demonstrated that they know their audience, they believe in their mission, and they take pride in the impact they can make on young lives.

Fourteen writers spent the month of July brainstorming ideas, generating potential plots, writing, revising, and providing critiques. Authoring quality books is challenging work, and these authors have our immense gratitude and respect: Rochelle, Destiney, Naseem, Darrin, Aderemi, Taijah, Abreona, Temil, Marques, Ericka, Dartavius, Dache, Kairon, and R.E.L.

These books represent a collaboration between Reach Incorporated and Shout Mouse Press, and we are grateful for the leadership provided by members of both teams. From Reach, D'Juan Thomas contributed meaningfully to discussions and morale, and the Reach summer program leadership kept us organized and well-equipped. From the Shout Mouse Press team, we thank Story Coach Hayes Davis and Story Scribes Sarai Johnson, Barrett Smith, Andi Mirviss, Eva Shapiro, and Rachel Page for bringing both fun and insight to the project. We can't thank enough illustrators Evey Cahall, Carson McNamara, Jamilla Okubo, and Zoe Gatti for bringing these stories to life with their beautiful artwork. We are grateful for the time and talents of these writers and artists!

Finally, we thank those of you who have purchased books and cheered on our authors. It is your support that makes it possible for these teen authors to engage and inspire young readers. We hope you smile as much while you read as these teens did while they wrote.

Mark Hecker,
Reach Incorporated

Kathy Crutcher,
Shout Mouse Press

About Reach Incorporated

Reach Incorporated develops grade-level readers and capable leaders by preparing teens to serve as tutors and role models for younger students, resulting in improved literacy outcomes for both.

Founded in 2009, Reach recruits high school students to be elementary school reading tutors. Elementary school students average 1.5 grade levels of reading growth per year of participation. This growth – equal to that created by highly effective teachers – is created by high school students who average more than two grade levels of growth per year of program participation.

As skilled reading tutors, our teens noticed that the books they read with their students did not reflect their reality. As always, we felt the best way we could address this issue was to let our teen tutors author new books. Through our collaboration with Shout Mouse Press, these teens create fanciful stories with diverse characters that invite young readers to explore the world through words. By purchasing our books, you support student-led, community-driven efforts to improve educational outcomes in the District of Columbia.

Learn more at www.reachincorporated.org.

CPSIA information can be obtained
at www.ICGtesting.com
Printed in the USA
LVOW06s1446131216

517084LV00040B/308/P

9 781945 434020